If You Lived When There Was Slavery in America

BY ANNE KAMMA

ILLUSTRATED BY PAMELA JOHNSON

SCHOLASTIC  NONFICTION

An Imprint of

SCHOLASTIC

New York   Toronto   London   Auckland   Sydney
Mexico City   New Delhi   Hong Kong   Buenos Aires

ISBN-13: 978-0-439-56706-0
ISBN-10: 0-439-56706-8

Text copyright © 2004 by Anne Kamma.
Illustrations copyright © 2004 by Pamela Johnson.

20 19 18 17   40   14/0

Printed in the U.S.A.
First printing, February 2004

Art Direction by Madalina Stefan Blanton
Book Design by David Neuhaus

For my mother

ACKNOWLEDGMENTS

With grateful thanks to the many helpful people at the National Park Service; Kay Cheyvert, LSU Rural Life Museum, LA; Carol and Roger Clark, Kingsley Plantation, FL; Carla Cowles, Selma to Montgomery National Historical Trail/Tuskegee; Kay Crank, Battenkill Books, Cambridge, NY; Laura Gates, Superintendent at Cane River Creole National Historical Park, LA; Ellen Levine; my editor, Eva Moore; Fraser Neiman, Director of Archaeology, Monticello, VA; Professor Marie Jenkins Schwartz, University of Rhode Island; Lou Sorkin, American Museum of Natural History, New York City; and Toby Yuen. This book makes extensive use of slave narratives. Among additional research material used, special mention should be made of the fine PBS series *Africans in America* and the book by the same name by Charles Johnson, Patricia Smith, and the WGBH Series Research Team. Both the film and the book proved especially valuable resources.

CONTENTS

Introduction

When the United States became a new nation in 1783, half a million people in the country were slaves. Most of them were farmworkers in the South.

A slave is someone who is owned by another person. Slaves were forced to work their whole lives without pay. Since a slave was thought of as a piece of property — like a cow or a chair — owners were allowed to do whatever they wanted with their slaves. They could whip them, sell them, or even work them to death.

The Declaration of Independence says that "all men are created equal." But when it was written in 1776, it was not meant for people who were slaves. Some states, like Vermont, did free their slaves then. Massachusetts outlawed slavery in 1783. And little by little, people in the North set their slaves free.

Most white people in the South wanted to keep their slaves. This was one of the reasons for the terrible war between the Northern states and the Southern states known as the Civil War. The Civil War started in 1861. By then, there were four million slaves living in the South. When the North won the war in 1865, all the slaves were freed, and slavery ended in America.

You will see that the years of slavery were a very sad time in American history. It is hard today to understand how a person could be "owned" by another person. But just as it is important to understand all the good things that have happened in America, it is important to understand when something bad, like slavery, happens. That way we can help make our future better than our past.

The color on this time line shows the years this book is mostly about.

1492	1505	1607	1619	1620	1783	1861	1865	1873–1888
Columbus discovers the Americas.	African slaves arrive in Hispaniola (now known as Haiti & Dominican Republic).	Jamestown, first British settlement in America.	First African captives arrive in Jamestown.	Pilgrims arrive in Plymouth.	America wins independence from England.	Civil War starts.	Civil War is over. Slavery ends in America.	Slavery ends in Puerto Rico, Cuba, and Brazil.

1505–1800s

African slaves are brought to Brazil, Mexico, Peru, and the Caribbean islands.

How do we know what it was like to be a slave?

We can't ask those who were slaves, because they died long ago. And yet we know a great deal from their own words, because thousands of ex-slaves told their stories.

Some wrote books after they escaped to freedom. So many people wanted to know what slavery was like that several of these books became bestsellers. Some former slaves told their stories to others who wrote them down.

The ex-slaves told about their families, the houses they lived in, the food they ate, and the clothing they wore. They told of their grief when a child was sold, of the hard work, and of the cruel whippings by slave owners. But they also told us about the games they played as children, their love for their parents, and some good times they had.

Olaudah Equiano (1745–1797) was kidnapped in Africa and sold into slavery at the age of eight. He later escaped and wrote about his life as a slave. He was in his late twenties when this portrait was painted.

Frederick Douglass (1817–1895) became very famous after writing his life story, which moved both white and black Americans to join the fight against slavery.

Susie King Taylor (1848–1912) was born in 1848 under the slave law in Georgia. She became a nurse and teacher during the Civil War and wrote a book about her life depicting how hard it was for her and other slaves to get an education.

Did the English use slaves when they first came to America?

In the beginning, the first English settlers didn't use slaves to do most of the hard work. They had indentured servants.

Indentured servants were usually poor men and women who wanted to leave England and come to America. But they didn't have money for the boat trip. So a deal was made with someone in America.

The deal was this: "If you pay for my boat trip, I'll work for you for four to seven years without pay. But when it's over, I'm free." Indentured servants were sometimes treated like slaves, especially during the early years of the

English settlements. Some were starved and beaten by the employers who "owned" them. They were not allowed to run away. And they could be sold to another employer. But once their servant time was up, they were free.

Why did slavery start in America?

Indentured servants were free to go when their servant time was up. Then the owner would have to pay for new indentured servants to come to America. And sometimes there weren't enough indentured servants for all the work that needed to be done.

It was cheaper to have slaves. Slaves worked their whole lives without pay. Anyone who owned slaves knew he would have enough workers, because slaves couldn't leave. And in those days, most people didn't think slavery was wrong.

At first, the English settlers tried to use Native Americans for slaves. But the Native Americans died of European diseases or ran away. So the English decided to use Africans instead. Spain and Portugal had already been using African slaves for more than a hundred years — in places like Hispaniola, Mexico, Puerto Rico, and Brazil.

Each year, more and more people in America owned slaves. Massachusetts was the first English colony to make slavery legal, in 1641. After a while, slavery was legal everywhere.

Were all slaves brought over from Africa?

At first, most were. More than half a million Africans were captured and brought to what is now the United States. Africans were also brought in from slave-owning colonies in the Caribbean and other places in South America.

As time passed, more and more slaves were born in America. When the United States became a nation in 1783, most people who were slaves had been born here. In 1808, it became against the law to bring in slaves from other countries. Now, when owners wanted more slaves, they bought slaves already living in the States.

United States

500,000 taken to United States

4 to 5 million taken to the Caribbean

Mexico

200,000 taken to Mexico

AFRICA

500,000 taken to the Guianas

The Guianas

ATLANTIC
OCEAN

From 1502 to 1870 about
12 million African people
were taken from their homeland
to be slaves in Europe and the Americas.

SOUTH
AMERICA

3.6 to 5 million taken to Brazil

Brazil

WHAT HAPPENED TO AFRICANS WHO WERE CAPTURED?

More than twenty million Africans were captured, mostly by enemy tribes. Half died during the long march from their village to the seaport. The rest were sold to Europeans and put on ships sailing to the Americas.

Hundreds of people were chained together with no place to move or stand up. Many died of disease or beatings, or went mad during the terrible sea voyage, known as the Middle Passage. Those who survived became slaves in North and South America and the Caribbean.

Where did American slaves live?

Most lived on farms called plantations.

Some plantations were small farms with only a few slaves. Others were very big, with hundreds of slaves. Most were in between. Crops such as cotton, tobacco, rice, or sugar were grown on the plantations. Owners could make a lot of money from these kinds of crops.

On the bigger plantations, the owner often lived in a fancy house called the Big House. Slaves lived in cabins in a section called the Quarters.

A big plantation was like a small village. Around the Big House were lots of little houses. In each house, special work was done — such as weaving cloth, sewing clothes, or making candles, soap, or shoes. Slaves made almost everything that was needed right there. There were also carpentry shops and blacksmith shops, all run by the slaves.

Some slaves lived in towns and big cities. They worked in factories and people's homes.

What was a cabin in the Quarters like?

Most cabins were small, with one or two rooms. Sometimes as many as twelve people — a whole family — lived in one cabin. This was where you ate, slept, and spent time together. George Kye, a slave in Oklahoma, remembered his house being so crowded, "you couldn't stir us with a stick!"

The cabin was dark inside, because there was only one small window. Slaves often didn't have candles. They used lighted pine knots instead, or grease lamps. You just poured some grease in a pan and lit it.

It was smoky in the cabins. The women cooked in pots hanging in an open fireplace. On winter nights, you had to keep the fire going to stay warm. To keep out the rain and cold, you stuffed cracks in the walls with rags and mud.

Where would you sleep?

If you were lucky, you slept in a bed. If not, you slept on the dirt floor on a mattress, or on some rags. People made their own mattresses. They stuffed the mattress sacks with cornhusks, straw, or soft moss, which the children gathered. For a pillow, you rolled up some clothing and tucked it under your head.

You would probably have only one blanket, so it was hard to keep warm on cold winter nights. In the morning, everyone pulled their mattresses off the floor and put them away.

Why did some cabins have tilted chimneys?

Many chimneys were made out of sticks and mud. If they caught fire, your whole house could burn down.

But somebody had a great idea. Why not build a different kind of chimney — a chimney that tilts away from the house? The chimney would be held up by poles.

This picture shows what the Quarters may have looked like on a Sunday. That was the day of the week field slaves didn't have to work. They could take care of their own household chores, go fishing, play music, and spend time together.

If there was a fire, all you had to do was rush outside and knock down the poles. *Bam!* The burning chimney would fall to the ground, away from the cabin. And your house would be safe.

So that's what many people did. In fact, some of the slave cabins at Monticello, the home of President Thomas Jefferson, had tilted chimneys.

What would you wear?

Every winter, owners handed out new clothes to their slaves. But often owners didn't give them enough clothes to wear, even though it was the slaves' hard work that made the owners rich.

Usually your clothes had to last you all year. If they wore out, you'd be wearing rags until you got new clothes.

Many boys and girls wore just long shirts. Sometimes owners gave boys pants to wear, and girls got skirts or dresses. Slave children rarely wore shoes, even when it rained or snowed. When you were about ten, you would start working in the fields or doing other adult work. That's when you got a pair of shoes, and maybe a warm jacket and socks. Children stopped wearing the long shirts at that age.

Slaves often went barefoot during the summer. That way they saved their shoes, so they'd be in good shape for the winter.

"We didn't have hardly any clothes, and most of the time they were just rags. We went barefoot until it got real cold. Our feet would crack open from the cold and bleed. We would sit down [and] bawl and cry because it hurt so. Mother made moccasins for our feet from old pants."
—*Emma Knight, a slave in Missouri*

What would you eat?

Every Sunday, you got some food from the plantation owner. It was the same food every week — bacon, corn-meal, and molasses. If you were a child, you got half of what an adult got until you were ready to work in the fields. This food had to last you a whole week.

Most of the time you ate hot cornmeal mush with molasses and bacon. You also ate ash cakes. These were like small, thick pancakes made of cornmeal and water. They were baked right in the fire. Before eating them, you had to scrape off the ashes.

Some owners gave their slaves better food, especially if they worked in the owner's house. But many slaves went hungry. Thomas Cole, a slave in Alabama, remembered one owner who fed his mules well, but kept his slaves half-starved.

How did people get extra food?

There were many ways to get extra food. But you had to do it at night and on Sundays — if you weren't too tired. Men and boys hunted for opossum and raccoons in the woods. Slaves weren't allowed to carry guns, so they used clubs and dogs. You always hoped your father would bring back an opossum, because then you could have delicious roasted 'possum and sweet potatoes.

Many slaves went fishing in nearby rivers and creeks. One man invented a fish trap that caught so many fish, he gave fish to all his friends.

Some owners let their slaves have a little piece of land for vegetables. And many raised chickens. Children helped out by trapping rabbits and picking wild nuts and berries in the woods.

Would you live with your father and mother?

Most young slave children lived with their parents. But sometimes parents had to live in two different places because they had two different owners. Then you would live with your mother.

After age ten, children were often sold away from their families. Younger children weren't usually sold. In some states, it was against the law to sell a young child away from his or her mother.

Slave parents loved their children and watched over them. During the day, slaves who were too old to go out into the fields looked after babies and the youngest children. Everyone else worked. You'd see your parents mostly in the mornings, late in the evenings, and on Sundays. Henry Barnes remembered staying awake at night, waiting for his mother to come home and tuck him in.

That little white gal was born rich and free,
She's the sap from out a sugar tree;
But you are just as sweet to me,
My little colored child.
— *from a slave mother's lullaby*

What if your father belonged to another slave owner?

If he lived nearby, your father could come and see you. But he might have to walk many miles at night to get there, sometimes through rivers and dark woods.

Perhaps he'd bring you food or blankets. Perhaps he'd go hunting or fishing with you on Sundays, so you would have opossum and fish for supper. One slave remembered that her dad chopped enough wood on Saturday evenings to last until Wednesday, when he came back.

If the slave owner didn't give permission, though, your dad could be in big trouble when he visited you. If caught, he could be whipped. But many slaves went anyway. They were willing to risk beatings so they could be with their families.

"My father was sold away from us when I was small. . . .
He would often slip back to our cottage at night. We would gather around him and crawl up in his lap, tickled slap to death, but he gave us these pleasures at a painful risk. When his Master missed him, he would beat him all the way home. We could track him the next day by the blood stains."
— *Hannah Chapman, a slave in Mississippi*

What would your name be?

Your father and mother might name you Sally or Ned, after a favorite grandparent. Or Kagne or Cuffy, after an African ancestor. Some children were named after the day of the week they were born on, just as many children in Africa were. Sometimes the owner gave children the names *he* wanted them to have.

Slaves could not use their own family names. They had to take the last names of their owners. So if your first name was Sally, and your owner's last name was Jones, your name was Sally Jones. If your owner sold you to someone named Maddox, your new name was Sally Maddox. You could have many last names in your life, one for each time you were sold. Many slaves were called only by their first names.

Some slaves also had secret names — especially if your parents didn't like the name the owner gave you. Then only you and the other slaves would know what it was.

What happened when slaves were sold?

Imagine if someone could take your mom or your dad away any time they wanted.

Imagine losing your sister or brother, and maybe never seeing them again.

Imagine if you were sold away from your family.

That's how terrible slavery was.

You were lucky if your new owner lived nearby. Then your family could see you on visits. But often slaves were sold to someone far away.

Some owners tried to keep slave families together. They knew that slaves with families worked harder and didn't run away. Others felt it was wrong to split up a family. Usually, though, owners sold slaves just to make money.

When an owner died, there was always a fear that your family would be split up. That's what happened most of the time. If you weren't sold, you would be given to someone in the dead owner's family — maybe his wife or his son. Your new "owner" could be much younger than you. In fact, he could be a baby.

"Children were separated from sisters and brothers and never saw one another again. Of course they cried. You think they didn't cry when they were sold like cattle? I could tell you about it all day, but even then you couldn't guess the awfulness of it."
— *Delia Garlic, a slave in Alabama*

When would you need a pass?

If you wanted to visit someone on another plantation, you would need a pass. If you lived in town and you had to go to the store, you'd need a pass. Slaves couldn't go anywhere without a pass.

A pass was a note written by the slave owner. It gave you permission to go somewhere. This is what it might say:

Henry has permission to go from my plantation to
Mr. Scott's, and return by 12 o'clock tonight.

Joseph Moore
January 1, 1850

What happened if you didn't have a pass?

You'd have to be careful the patrollers didn't catch you! It was the patrollers' job to look for slaves traveling without passes. If a slave didn't have a pass, the patroller whipped him — sometimes so hard his back was bloody, and he was so sore he couldn't work for days.

Many slaves were caught when they slipped off to visit family or friends at a nearby plantation. But a slave could also get caught in town. Then the patrollers might take him to a fenced-in area, tie him to a post, and whip him there.

Slaves used all kinds of tricks to fool the patrollers. Some dragged bushes behind them to wipe out their footprints. That way the patrollers couldn't track them. Tom Holland remembered how slaves at his plantation pretended to be so tired at night that the patrollers thought they had all gone right to sleep. As soon as they knew the patrollers weren't watching, they sneaked out.

Would you go to school?

No, slave children weren't allowed to go to school.

That's why most slaves couldn't read and write, or count and do arithmetic. Most had never seen a map of the United States, or of the world.

If you were lucky, you could go to a secret school. You'd sneak out of the Quarters at night and go far into the woods. Here a fellow slave would teach you and other slaves whatever he knew. Or you might try and find someone to teach you alone.

Slave children also learned by listening to songs and stories told in the Quarters. You might hear a story about an African ancestor brought here long ago, or what life was like in Africa. Stories about Brer Rabbit were popular because he always outsmarted the powerful fox, just as slaves sometimes found ways to outsmart their owners.

Did some owners teach their slaves to read?

Yes, a few. Some owners wanted their slaves to read the Bible. Others wanted their slaves to be able to read so they could do their jobs better. Still others just believed slaves should know how to read. An owner who taught his own slave to read wasn't punished, even if that was against the law. In many states, a white person could go to jail if he or she taught someone else's slave to read.

Phillis Wheatley, a seven-year-old slave girl from Africa, was taught more than just reading. Her Boston owners also taught her history, geography, astronomy, and English and Latin literature before they freed her.

When Phillis was about sixteen, a book of her poems was published in England. Many people didn't believe that a black person could have written such a great book, but she proved them all wrong. She became world-famous.

Library of Congress

Most often, though, it was white children who taught their black playmates how to read — usually in secret. Mandy Jones was a slave boy in Mississippi. He remembered how the white children would slip off after school and secretly teach the black children what they had just learned.

"[The owner's son Crosby] . . . took a great liking to me. Once in an undertone he asked how I would like to have an education. I was overjoyed . . . and he at once began to teach me secretly. . . . He furnished me books and slipped all the papers he could get me, and I was the best educated Negro in the community without anyone except the slaves knowing what was going on."
— *Robert Glenn, a slave in North Carolina*

Why weren't slaves allowed to read and write?

Owners were afraid that if slaves could read and write, they would write fake passes.

If you had a fake pass, you could fool the patrollers. They wouldn't know if you were visiting someone without permission — or if you were running away.

Most owners also thought learning to read and write gave slaves a bad attitude. Owners wanted slaves who obeyed and didn't complain. They didn't want slaves who were "too smart and harder to manage," as one ex-slave said.

In 1831, Nat Turner led a slave revolt that killed fifty-seven whites. Turner was caught and killed, but whites knew that he had been a preacher who knew how to read and write. They decided that slaves who could read and write were dangerous. So they passed strict new laws to punish anyone who tried to teach slaves.

Were slaves punished for knowing how to read?

Yes, many slaves were whipped cruelly. Some were sold as soon as the owner found out they could read.

You could be punished for just holding a book, or looking in one. Elijah Green, a slave in South Carolina, remembered that being caught with pencil and paper "was a major crime."

Owners tried hard to keep young children from learning to read. One little boy was given a whipping because he and some white children were playing with ABC blocks.

What kind of work did slaves do?

All kinds. Wherever there was work to be done, you were likely to find slaves.

They worked in people's houses and in factories. They built bridges and railroads, and dug canals. In many places, they were pioneers, because they cleared wild land for new settlements, and drained swamps to make rice fields. But most slaves did farm work. If you worked on a big plantation, you'd plant and harvest tobacco or sugar. Every slave feared working in the flooded rice fields. It was very hot, and you had to stand in water all day long. You could get bitten by water bugs and snakes. Many workers got sick and died.

Slaves who had special skills, such as carpenters and mechanics, could make money if they had time off. Carpenters made furniture and sold it, and shoemakers made shoes. If you saved enough money, you might even buy yourself and be free.

Did slaves have to work very hard?

Yes, terribly hard—especially if they worked on plantations. Slaves used to say that they worked "from can see, to can't." As long as there was daylight to see by, they had to work.

It didn't matter if it was freezing cold or pouring rain, or just plain hot. Work didn't stop.

When the wake-up horn blew in the morning, it was still dark outside. You got up and hurried through breakfast. By the time the second horn blew, you'd better be standing in the field ready to work. Otherwise the slave driver gave you a bad whipping.

After you worked hard for six or seven hours, the lunch horn blew. That's when you finally had a short rest and ate your corn cakes and bacon. When it was too dark to see, everyone headed home to cook dinner and do their chores. But you had to be in bed by nine o'clock. The slave driver came around to check on you. He wanted to make sure you were getting enough sleep, so that you could work hard the next day, too.

"If I had my life to live over, I would die fighting rather than be a slave again. . . . All we knew was work, and hard work. We were taught to say 'yes, sir!' and scrape down and bow, and to do just exactly what we were told to do, made no difference if we wanted to or not."
— *Robert Falls, a slave in Tennessee*

Did the children have to work?

Yes. Young children had chores — like feeding the chickens and sweeping the yard. As you got older, you might drive the cows to pasture, or bring water and wood to the kitchen.

Booker T. Washington was only seven when he rode a horse carrying heavy bags of corn to the mill. If the bags fell off on the way, he had to wait until an adult came by and helped him put the bags back on the horse.

Many children worked in the owner's house. You'd help scrub the floors, polish the brass, and fan the flies away while the owner's family ate dinner. Girls, sometimes as young as four, took care of the owner's small children. One little slave girl had her own way of stopping the babies' screaming in the middle of the night. She just started screaming right along with them until they finally stopped!

In the fields, it was the children's job to pick all the worms off the tobacco plants. The overseer watched everyone, and if you missed some, he made you bite each worm in half as a punishment.

When you had grown enough, usually between ten and twelve years old, everything changed. Now you were ready to work long hours with the adults.

"When I was six, I carried water. When I got to be seven years old, I was cutting sprouts like a man, and when I was eight, I could pick one hundred pounds of cotton."
— Mary Island, *a slave in Louisiana*

Was there time for play?

Some children under ten worked so hard that there was little time for play. But many did play after they finished their chores. Older slave children played games around the plantations, in the woods, and on the streets.

Often, white and black children played together. Some were even friends. When Frederick Douglass was a slave boy playing on the streets of Baltimore and it was time to choose partners, he remembered being chosen as often as a white boy. Another slave boy never let his white play-mates win at games, even when they were the sons of the slave owner.

"It was a long time before I knew myself to be a slave. . . . The first seven or eight years of the slave boy's life are about as full of sweet content as those of the most favored and petted white children of the slaveholder . . . freed from all restraint, the slave boy can be, in his life and conduct, a genuine boy, doing whatever his boyish nature suggests."
— *Frederick Douglass*

Many slaves remembered this as a happy time. Some young children didn't even know they were slaves, because they felt so free. Harriet Jacobs didn't realize she was a slave until she was six years old. Sam Aleckson didn't realize it until he was ten.

It was a jolt to suddenly learn you were not free like the other children.

What games would you play?

You'd play hide and seek, hopscotch, jump rope, and lots of other games.

Slaves were usually much too poor to buy toys. So the children made their own. They made dolls out of rags. When they needed marbles, they rolled balls of clay and dried them in the sun.

Lizzie Davis remembered that "everybody was crazy to ride on the flying mare." The children made it themselves out in the woods. It looked like a seesaw, but it didn't go up and down. It spun around in a circle. When someone gave you a shove, you went flying!

How did slaves help one another?

Slaves helped one another in all kinds of ways. They might:

— Sneak food to someone who had run away and was living in the woods or swamps.

— Become "family" to a child who was separated from his parents.

— Write a fake pass for a slave who couldn't write.

— Give some of their cotton to a slow picker, so he or she didn't get whipped for coming up short.

— Share the food they got from hunting and fishing.

"I was just a little thing; taken away from my mammy and pappy when I needed them the most. The only caring that I knew about was given me by a friend of my pappy. His name was John White. My pappy told him to take care of me for him. John was a fiddler, and many a night I woke up to find myself asleep between his legs while he was playing for a dance for the white folks."
— *Mingo White, a slave in Alabama*

What rule did every slave child learn?

Every slave child was taught this rule: Never tell the owner, or any white person, what goes on in the Quarters.

You could cause great harm without meaning to. You might talk about a slave who was planning to run away. If the owner knew, he would beat the slave, or even sell him.

Or you might talk about a slave who was making secret trips to see his family at another plantation. That could get the person whipped.

Sometimes owners gave treats to children for spying on grown-ups in the Quarters. If you were caught spying, you were punished. It was important that you learn never to do that again. Everyone's safety depended on your keeping your mouth zipped.

Were slaves allowed to get married?

When a man and woman fell in love, they had to go to their owners to get permission to marry. Usually the owners gave them permission. But sometimes they didn't — especially if the slaves had two different owners. Then the slaves might decide to have a secret marriage in the Quarters.

But there were no laws to protect a slave marriage. An owner could break up a marriage any time he wanted. At slave weddings, the bride and groom weren't allowed to promise that they'd stay together "until death do us part."

Most of the time, though, owners liked having their slaves marry. They thought married slaves didn't run away as often. And the more children the slaves had, the richer the owners became. Some owners made more money selling their slaves than they did selling their crops.

A wedding was a happy time in the Quarters, with lots of food and dancing.

"Exter made me a wedding ring . . . out of a big red button with his pocketknife . . . It was so smooth that it looked like a red satin ribbon tied around my finger. That sure was a pretty ring. I wore it about fifty years, then it got so thin that I lost it one day in the washtub when I was washing clothes."
— *Tempie Herndon Durham, a slave in North Carolina*

What was "jumping the broom"?

Slaves had a special way to celebrate a marriage — they "jumped the broom." One former slave remembered that "they just laid down the broom on the floor, and the couple joined hands and jumped backward over the broomstick."

Sometimes the broom was raised off the ground. That made it harder, because you weren't supposed to touch the broom as you jumped. Touching it was thought to bring you bad luck.

What was the best time of the year?

Christmastime was the best. That's when slaves finally had some time off. For a week between Christmas and New Year's, work slowed down for house slaves, or stopped altogether for field slaves. It was a time for dancing and Christmas presents and the best eating you had all year.

There would also be religious services and lots of visiting. At Christmas, slave owners handed out passes so those with family members who lived nearby could travel and see them. Even if your father lived on a different plantation or had been hired out to work away from home, chances are he'd be back at Christmastime.

What was the first thing you'd say on Christmas Day?

The first time you saw a friend or relative on Christmas Day, you'd yell "Christmas Gif'!" The trick was to yell it out before the other person did, because then he had to give you a present. If your friend yelled "Christmas Gif'!" first, you had to give *him* a present. So you had to be quick.

The presents weren't fancy — just nuts or little tea cakes. But everyone had lots of fun whether they won or lost.

"Christmas Gif'" was a game invented by slaves, but it soon spread to the Big House. James Bolton, a slave in Arkansas, remembered how everybody ran up to the Big House early Christmas morning and hollered out "Morning, Christmas Gif'!" The slave owner got "caught" this way, then handed out presents to everyone.

How would you find out the latest news?

There were lots of ways, but you had to make sure the owner didn't catch you doing it.

If you went into town for your master's mail, you could listen at the post office while white people talked about the letters they had received. That was a really good way to get news.

House slaves kept their ears open while they worked in the Big House. If you heard that an owner had money trouble, that was terrible news, because slaves might be sold to pay the debt. Many slaves ran away when they found out they were going to be sold.

If you knew how to read, you could look at newspapers while working in the owner's house. But you had to do it quickly. Slaves caught reading were punished.

As soon as you heard any news, you passed it along. Sometimes you had to send messages in a secret way — maybe by singing a certain song. If you sang "Steal Away to Jesus," for example, other slaves would know there was going to be a secret religious meeting in the woods that night.

Why was corn shucking fun?

Slaves weren't allowed to leave the plantation very often. So it was fun when there was a chance to get together with others from nearby plantations. For many grown-ups and children, the most fun came at corn-shucking time.

After the harvest, the corn was put in huge piles, sometimes as high as a house. At lunchtime, slaves from other plantations came over to help shuck the corn. Shucking means pulling the outside leaves off the corncob.

Sometimes hundreds of people worked in two teams to see which would be first to finish their pile. There would be singing and joking as the shucked corn was thrown high in the air, landing behind the teams.

Each plantation had its own corn shucking, so you might go to ten or twelve corn shuckings in one year!

Prince Johnson remembered that when his team won "we put our Captain on our shoulders and rode him up and down while everybody cheered and clapped their hands like the world was coming to an end."

As soon as the shucking was done, the party began.

The owner provided all kinds of delicious foods, like roast pork, and drink. After eating until they were stuffed, everybody joined in dancing the "Turkey Trot," "Buzzard Lope," and "Mary Jane" until morning.

Were any black people free?

Yes, many. Most blacks were still slaves, but by 1860 there were about 488,000 free blacks living in America. Nearly half lived in the slave states in the South.

Most free blacks were not wealthy, but April Ellison was. After he bought his freedom, he opened a successful cotton gin repair shop in South Carolina. He also became a planter, owning more than three hundred acres of good farmland.

If you were free, you had a chance to go to school, even if you lived in the South.

Many free blacks, like the great leader Frederick Douglass, who escaped from slavery on a Maryland plantation, worked to end slavery.

William Still was a free black man living in Philadelphia. One of the runaway slaves he helped turned out to be his long-lost brother, Peter!

How could you become free?

The easiest way was if your mother was free, because then you would be born free. Even if your father was a slave, you'd still be free. You could also be freed by the slave owner. He might reward you for serving him. George Washington arranged to have all his slaves freed after he and his wife died. Most owners, though, didn't free their slaves.

Venture Smith did what some slaves did — he bought his own freedom with money saved doing extra work. Slaves who had special skills, like carpenters and machinists, had an easier time making extra money. As soon as Venture Smith was free, he started saving again. This time he bought his wife, Meg, and their three children. Now the whole family was free.

This didn't always work out because some owners cheated. They took your money but then never set you free.

Could you be made a slave even if you were free?

If you were a free black, there was always a chance that you might be kidnapped. Kidnappers could grab you and sell you to someone far away. Then you'd be a slave.

Kidnappers were criminals. It was against the law to kidnap a free black person. But they did it anyway, because they made a lot of money. As soon as they caught you, the kidnappers changed your name. That made it harder for your family to find you. If you tried to tell the new slave owner that you were free, you were whipped and told never to talk about it again.

That's what happened to Solomon Northup of New York. He had been free all his life, but he was kidnapped and sold to a Louisiana slave owner. After a long time, he finally got word to friends and New York officials and was released. When he returned home to his joyful family, his daughter didn't even recognize him as he walked in the door. He had been away for twelve years.

"It's bad to belong to folks that own you soul and body."
— *Delia Garlic, a slave in Alabama*

Was it dangerous to run away?

It was very dangerous. Slaves who were caught were beaten badly, or even killed. Owners paid big rewards for capturing runaways, so slave hunters were everywhere.

Leaving on a Sunday could give you a head start, because the owner might not know you were gone until work started Monday morning. The first thing you had to worry about was being caught by the slave hunters' dogs. So you rubbed onion or hot pepper on your shoes to get the dogs off your scent. And you walked in the creek where the dogs couldn't smell you.

$100 REWARD
FOR RETURN OF MY
SLAVE MARIANNE.
DARK SKINNED MAN...

Owners put out ads describing what runaways looked like. So some slaves wore disguises, like false mustaches. Men dressed like women, and women like men. One girl was only fifteen when she escaped dressed as a boy. Her disguise was so good that even people helping her thought she was a boy.

Slaves found all sorts of ways to escape. Some hid in vegetable wagons, on steamships, or stole the owner's horse for a fast getaway. Henry "Box" Brown got in a box and mailed himself to freedom! But most walked, often hundreds of miles.

Along the way, they were helped by people who hated slavery. They were called *abolitionists* because they wanted to *abolish*, or end, this terrible practice. Some abolitionists were white people, some were black. Although many runaways were caught, by 1861 more than sixty thousand slaves had escaped to freedom in the North.

What was the Underground Railroad?

In 1832, a slave named Tice Davids ran away and headed north to freedom. His owner tried hard to catch him, but after a while Davids just seemed to have vanished. "He must have gone on an underground railroad!" the surprised slave owner said. The name caught on. Soon everyone was talking about how slaves were escaping on the Underground Railroad.

Of course it wasn't a real railroad. It was the name for the secret way that slaves were helped to get out of the South and to freedom in the North. The people who helped slaves along the way were called railroad workers. Houses that hid slaves were called stations. And the people who fed you and gave you a place to sleep were called station masters. When you were ready to travel on, the people who led you to the next station were called conductors. One of the most famous conductors on the Underground Railroad was Harriet Tubman.

What happened during the Civil War?

When the war began in 1861, many slaves ran away to join the Northern Army. They believed that if the North won the war, slavery would end.

During the war, in 1863, President Lincoln freed all the slaves living in states fighting against the North. This was called the Emancipation Proclamation. The South had declared itself a new country, so it didn't obey this new Northern law. But word spread among the slaves, and even more ran away. Freedom was in the air. Sometimes whole families fled together, walking at night to avoid the patrollers.

When they reached a Northern Army camp, many were put to work — and were paid for it. They dug trenches, built roads, repaired equipment, and did other war work. In addition, 180,000 men fought as soldiers in all-black units. Women nursed the wounded, cooked, and did the laundry. Some, like Harriet Tubman, became spies for the Northern Army.

During the four years of the war, half a million slaves ran away to freedom.

"Daddy was down at the creek. He jumped right in the water up to his neck. He was so happy he just kept on scooping up handfuls of water and dumping it on his head and yelling, 'I'm free! I'm free!'"
— *Louisa Bowes Rose, a slave in Virginia*

What was the first thing you would do when slavery ended?

When slavery ended, your life as a free person began. But the first thing you'd do is look for your family. Many slaves had been sold away. Now was the time to get your family back.

If your family lived on nearby plantations, it was easy to find them. One father rushed over to get his young daughter as soon as freedom came. Her mistress promised to school the girl if she could keep her, but the father put his daughter on his mule and rode away in the night.

Many slaves had been sold several times. That made it hard to track them down. You might have ended up in Texas, while your father and mother lived in Florida and Georgia. One way to search was to put ads in newspapers.

An ad might say:

Information wanted on my children, Lucy and David. When last heard from, they belonged to Bill Smith of Athens, Texas. Please send information to this newspaper. Isaac Jones

Some spent years looking for their families. Their powerful love gave them strength to keep going. Many slaves were lucky and did find one another again.

When did slavery end?

When the Civil War was over in 1865, the Thirteenth Amendment was added to the Constitution. It made slavery illegal.

The terrible time of slavery had finally ended in America.

"I looked at my hands to see if I was the same person. There was such a glory over everything. The sun came like gold through the trees, and over the fields, and I felt like I was in Heaven."
— *Harriet Tubman, upon becoming free*

You and your family can visit museums to learn more about how slaves lived and even see actual slave homes. Here are some places to visit.

Booker T. Washington National Monument
12130 Booker T. Washington Highway
Hardy, VA 24101
540-721-2094
www.nps.gov/bowa

Cane River Creole National Historical Park
400 Rapides Drive
Natchitoches, LA 71457
318-356-8441
www.nps.gov/cari

Colonial Williamsburg
P.O. Box 1776
Williamsburg, VA 23187-1776
1-800-History
www.colonialwilliamsburg.com

Kingsley Plantation
11676 Palmetto Avenue
Jacksonville, FL 32226
904-251-3537
www.nps.gov/timu

LSU Rural Life Museum
4650 Essen Lane
Baton Rouge, LA 70898
225-765-2437
http://rurallife.lsu.edu/

Monticello
P.O. Box 316
Charlottesville, VA 22902
434-984-9822
www.monticello.org

Natchez National Historical Park
1 Melrose Montebello Parkway
Natchez, MS 39120
601-446-5790
www.nps.gov/natc